Bob the Builder

Best in Show!

adapted by
Sonali Fry

based on a book by
Iona Treahy

SIMON SPOTLIGHT
New York   London   Toronto   Sydney   Singapore

Based upon the television series *Bob the Builder*™ created by HIT Entertainment PLC
and Keith Chapman, as seen on Nick Jr.® Photos by Hot Animation.

SIMON SPOTLIGHT
An imprint of Simon & Schuster Children's Publishing Division
1230 Avenue of the Americas,
New York, New York 10020

Manufactured in the United States of America

First Edition

2 4 6 8 10 9 7 5 3 1

ISBN 0-689-85720-9

Bob and the machines had an important job to do: They were going
to build a barn for Farmer Pickles's sheep!
At Farmer Pickles's farm, Roley made the ground nice and smooth,
ready for the barn to stand on.

Then Bob heard something. It sounded like a whistle.
The sound came again, and when he looked over the hedge, Bob
saw Farmer Pickles and his dog, Scruffty.

Farmer Pickles was training Scruffty to shake, sit, and roll over.

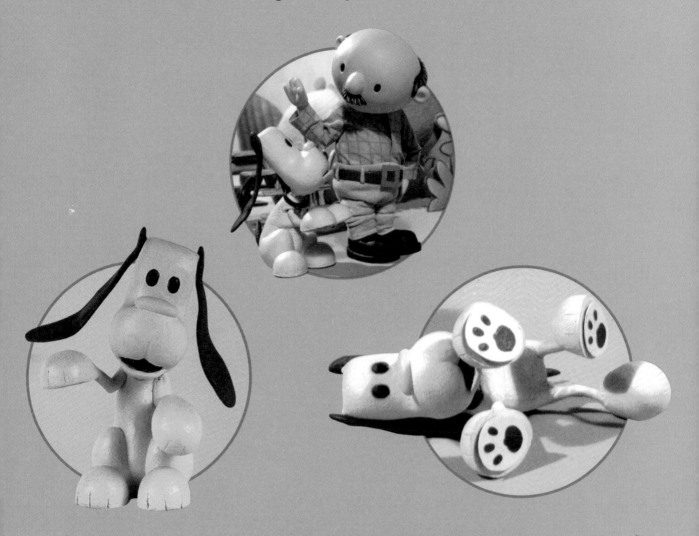

"Well done, you two!" said Bob.

"Ruff!" barked Scruffty, feeling pleased with himself.

"I have high hopes that Scruffty will win the dog show today," said Farmer Pickles proudly.

"Hey!" said Scoop. "How about entering Pilchard in the show? She's just as smart as Scuffty. I bet she could win."

"Ho, ho!" Farmer Pickles chuckled. "I'm sorry, Scoop, but it's a *dog* show."

Now Scoop wanted Pilchard to be in the show more than ever. He went back to the yard to look for her.

"Pilchard!" Scoop called. "Piiil-chaaard!"

Pilchard came out, wondering what all the noise was about.

"There, see?" said Scoop. "You came when I called you. Good girl!"

"Meow!" replied Pilchard.

"Now, let's try it again," said Scoop. "Here, Pilchard!" But this time Pilchard didn't move—not even a whisker.

Scoop remembered how Farmer Pickles had whistled to Scruffty. Scoop made a whistling noise through his exhaust pipe, but Pilchard still didn't move!

"Hmmm," said Scoop, feeling disappointed.

On the othe[...] [m]achines had almost
finished the b[...] and Lofty was moving
the third one [...]

"That's it, I[...]. A bit closer now. . . .
That's it, and [...]

Lofty place[...]y as he could.

"Well done[...] [A]ndy began to screw the
wall into plac[...]

Meanwhile, Scoop hadn't given up on his plan. He persuaded Pilchard to sit in his scoop, and off they went to the dog show.

When they got to the site of the dog show, they were all alone.
Scoop whistled for Pilchard to come. She put one paw toward Scoop,
but then she saw a mouse and ran straight past him.

"Piiil-chaaard!" called Scoop. But Pilchard kept chasing the mouse. "Please come back, Pilchard," said Scoop. "We don't have much time before the show."

Scoop followed Pilchard, but as he moved forward, he got tangled in the flags and banner. Scoop tried to free himself, but he got even more trapped!

"Oh, no!" called Scoop. "Help, Pilchard—I'm stuck!"

Pilchard ran to Farmer Pickles's farm for help.

"That's it, Lofty. Steady!" said Bob as Pilchard tried to get Wendy's attention.

"Meow!" said Pilchard loudly, sticking her paw out.

"Uh—I think she wants us to follow her," said Wendy.

"Let's go!" said Bob as they took off after Pilchard.

Pilchard raced ahead and led them to Scoop.

"Well done, Pilchard!" said Scoop with a big smile on his face.

"Can we fix it?" said Bob.

"Yes, we can!" shouted the others as Lofty pulled the flags and banner off of Scoop.

"Thanks, everyone!" said Scoop. "And you know something?" he asked Pilchard. "If they *did* let cats enter dog shows, you'd be the winner for sure."

Since Pilchard had been such a clever cat, Bob asked Mrs. Percival, who was one of the judges, if it would be all right for a cat to enter the dog show.

"It's a most unusual request, Bob," said Mrs. Percival. "But it may be possible," she said as she went to see what she could do.

A little while later the show was underway. Farmer Pickles and Scruffty were the first owner and dog to compete. Scruffty performed perfectly.

After all the dogs had been in the ring, Mrs. Percival announced
the final contestants—Scoop and Pilchard!
The judges watched very carefully.

Scoop whistled loudly.

Pilchard walked forward, sat down, and even rolled over. And to everyone's surprise—including Scoop's—she finished with a fancy flip!

The audience clapped and cheered.

"You have yourself an extremely smart cat there, Bob," said
Farmer Pickles admiringly.

"And you've got a very talented dog," replied Bob as he patted
Scruffty's head.

While the judges were making their decision, Bob and the
team went to congratulate Pilchard and Scoop.

"That was amazing, Pilchard!" said Scoop.

"Well done, Pilchard," said Bob.

"Meow!" said Pilchard.

Everyone lined up for the award ceremony. There was silence as Mrs. Percival entered the ring holding a trophy for the winner.

"I'm pleased to announce that the winners of this year's show
are Scoop and Pilchard!" said Mrs. Percival.

Bob, Wendy, and the machines all cheered, and Scruffty
wagged his tail.

Scoop felt very proud when Mrs. Percival placed the trophy
in Pilchard's paws.

"I knew you could do it!" said Scoop to Pilchard. "You're the
best in show!"

Pilchard replied, **"Meow!"**